JESSICA'S STORY

BY

PAMELA GOMEZ

ISBN 978-1-968970-34-5 (Paperback)
ISBN 978-1-968970-35-2 (Ebook)

Inquiries and Book Orders should be addressed to:

Leavitt Peak Press
17901 Pioneer Blvd Ste L #298, Artesia, California 90701
Phone #: 2092191548

Dr. Albert La Madrid said good-bye to little Stevie and went into his office. He sat down on his chair and breathed a sigh of relief. That was his last patient for the day. He was really tired. While he was busy every day, today had been an exception. Several people had just dropped in without making an appointment, and to make matters worse, his nurse left early because she became ill. But, oh well, it was over now - or so he thought.

Karen, his receptionist, entered into his office and spoke in a hushed voice, "I'm sorry, Dr. La Madrid, but Mrs. Ward is here with Jessica. They have an ex-ray with them that was taken over at St. John's Hospital. Mrs. Ward says that Jessica's arm is broken. She apologized for showing up so late but evidently, they just left the hospital. What shall I tell her?" Exasperated, Dr. LaMadrid ran his hands through his hair then looked at Karen and said, "Put her in Room 1, please. I'll be right there."

While Karen guided Jessica and her mother into Room 1, Dr. LaMadrid thought, *Hadn't he seen Jessica last week for a pulled muscle? Well, seven is a very awkward age,* he reasoned. He walked into Room 1 and saw Jessica seated next to her mother. He noticed right away that Jessica was in a tremendous amount of pain. She was grasping her left arm with her right one as if to support it. Her big blue eyes were filled with fear and pain, but Dr. LaMadrid observed that she wasn't crying.

"What happened, Jessica?" Dr. LaMadrid asked.

"She fell down the stairs," Jessica's mother answered quickly.

"Hmm," Dr. LaMadrid mused. "How did you do that?" He continued to look at her arm but watched her face very closely as well.

Jessica stared sullenly at the ceiling and then glancing down, mumbled, "It was an accident. I just wasn't watching where I was going."

"Thank you so much for seeing us Dr. LaMadrid," Mrs. Ward said. "Jessica feels so much better having her own doctor to take care of her. We really appreciate it."

"Oh no problem, " he said aloud then thought to himself, *It really isn't a problem."* This was one of those rare moments that made him very glad he had decided to become a pediatrician, though after the day he had, he wasn't sure why. He studied the ex-ray for a moment, then turned and spoke to Jessica. "We are going to need a cast on your arm. I will be as gentle as possible, okay?"

Jessica nodded slowly, her lips pursed with determination. But her frightened gaze never left Dr. LaMadrid's eyes.

"Can I lift you up onto this table, Jessica?" Dr. LaMadrid asked.

"Yes, thank you," she answered shyly.

Dr. LaMadrid gently lifted Jessica onto the examining table then proceeded to put her cast on.

Dr. La Madrid, with painstaking care, moistened and applied the strips of gauze that slowly began to take the shape of a cast. He smoothed the rough areas and leveled the surface between her thumb and index finger. He couldn't help but notice that Jessica had not taken her eyes off of him. He was gentler than he had ever been, and he was sure Jessica sensed this. Slowly, the fear that had been so obvious in Jessica's eyes began to disappear.

When Dr. LaMadrid finished setting the cast, he patted Jessica's head then remarked to her mother, "Your daughter was very brave through the entire thing. She never made a sound."

"She is my very good girl. Aren't you, honey?" Jessica's mother commented.

Dr. La Madrid observed the look that crossed Jessica's face as her mother spoke. *What was that look, he wondered? Was it relief that the pain was over or embarrassment that she had done something she should be ashamed of? No,* he decided, *it was something else. Could that have been fear he saw cross her face?*

Maybe, but what would she need to be afraid of now? Dr. La Madrid had a very uneasy feeling as he watched Mrs. Ward lead Jessica out of the office. *Had he seen Jessica flinch as her mother's arm went around her? No,* he determined, *maybe I am just really tired.* He assured himself, *you're probably overreacting.* Still, when he left his office that night, he had a strange feeling that something was wrong with that situation. And though he didn't know exactly how, he felt he would be playing a role in discovering just what it was.

When Dr. La Madrid opened his front door that evening, Jessica left his thoughts for a moment. His dog, Ernie, raced through the house at breakneck speed and leapt into his arms. As Albert wrestled with his pet, his doleful look became one with amused playfulness. Albert loved his springer spaniel, and it was very obvious the same held true for Ernie. They romped together for a few moments, until Albert's wife appeared in the doorway.

"Your dinner is ready, Albert. Are you hungry?" Suzanne asked. Before he had time to respond, she saw something in his face and asked, "What's wrong, dear? Did you have a rough day?"

"Oh yes, I did," he answered wearily. "Let me wash my hands first, then I'll tell you about it over dinner."

As Albert ate his re-heated dinner, he shared the Jessica incident with his wife. Suzanne became very quiet for a moment, then commented, "Do you think there is something to be concerned about?"

"I don't know, but for some reason, I can't seem to get it out of my mind," Albert responded.

"Well, you've had a very stressful day. Perhaps after you've had a good night's sleep you'll feel differently," Suzanne concluded.

Albert wasn't so sure. In fact, he couldn't concentrate on reading his magazine that night; the harder he tried, the more his mind wandered. He kept seeing little Jessica's face on every page.

Those big, beautiful blue eyes; and what an incredible shade of blue they were, too! They were probably close to azure in color, but it seemed at times they were almost transparent. While her eyes certainly stood out, she really had the look of an average seven-year-old. Her permanent teeth were just beginning to show, with her curly blonde hair generally having that unkempt look. Not too delicate nor too athletic looking. Why couldn't he just let go of this? Then he began thinking about Jessica's mother.

Mrs. Ward was a very attractive young woman who appeared to be around 35 years old. Her hair and make-up were always perfect, and she was always impeccably dressed. *They probably lived very comfortably,* he surmised. From what Mrs. Ward had told him, they had only lived in Fountain for a few months. Actually, this was only the third time he had seen Jessica. Whatever it was that he had felt this third time hadn't taken long to do it. Albert looked at the clock and moaned softly. It was eleven thirty and he was still awake.

He had another full day scheduled tomorrow, beginning with a cesarean section at 7:00 A.M. His thoughts then drifted to his own life.

He looked at his wife sleeping soundly next to him and wondered, *will we ever be fortunate enough to have a child of our own*? It had been the last thing on their minds at first. They had married while he was still in medical school and there was neither the time nor the finances for a family. Then came his internship - even less time and less money. When he started his own practice things slowly began to turn around. Still not much time, but at least the financial status had improved enough to entertain thoughts of having a baby.

That was 5 years ago and since then, they had been through every test imaginable to determine why they couldn't conceive. All the tests were inconclusive. It seemed there was no valid reason why they couldn't have a child. "Give it time," the specialists had said. So they waited, and waited, and tried not to place too much importance on it, which, of course, was next to impossible.

He would see the wistful look on his wife's face when she would see a newborn. He had heard her cry herself to sleep many, many nights. Though he felt ready for a family, it had never bothered him to that extent. Until now. It seemed like when he saw babies now, he began to think he and Suzanne would never become parents. And while they were on the waiting list for adopting a child, the agencies' parting words had been, "These things take time. It may be several years, so you need to relax and be prepared to wait - your time will come." Those words were so easy for others to say. *If they could only see it from our side*, he thought.

He had thought medical school was tough. He thought all the sacrifices he had made to open his own practice had been tough. But nothing had prepared him for this. It was, without question, the most emotionally draining experience of his life. But most people would wait; they also continued to wait. What else could they do?

As a sigh escaped his weary body, his final thoughts were of Jessica. He saw those eyes in front of him and reflected. I hope her parents realize how very fortunate they are to have that precious little girl. Albert's eyes slowly closed and he fell into a disturbing sleep.

CHAPTER TWO

THE PAIN!

Jessica flinched as a sharp pain bolted up her left arm. Jessica's mother caught her look and asked anxiously, "What happened, honey?"

"Nothing mother. I'm okay" Jessica replied. "Is it alright if I go to my room and lie down for a while? I'm really tired."

"Sure you can. If you need anything, just call for me," Jessica's mom said. "I'm going to make dinner for your father. He'll be home soon."

Jessica went toward the stairs that led to her bedroom and stopped abruptly. She drew in a breath and slowly ascended the steps as a tear threatened to slide down her cheek. She went into her room and laid down on the bed. She moved her sling around, then gingerly slipped her pillow under her cast. *Oh, that felt much better,* she thought. She wanted that horrible throbbing to stop. It hadn't hurt that badly at the doctor's office. Dr. LaMadrid was so nice. And he was gentle, too. But the pain was really setting in now. She wanted to cry but she knew she couldn't.

What if her mother came up to check on her? Or her dad? He would be home any minute. Jessica hadn't seen her dad for five days. She didn't want him to see her like this. No, she wouldn't cry. Maybe she should do her homework. She was in such pain though, and she knew she couldn't concentrate on school.

She leaned back against the headboard and closed her eyes. She thought, *I wonder how long we're going to live in this town?* Jessica and her parents had moved here to Fountain, California right after Christmas. They moved from Los Angeles, which was about an hour's drive away, so it hadn't been too complicated this time. Her father worked with computers and consequently, he needed to spend periods of time in different areas of the country. Her dad was very good at what he did. They had moved three times within the last year. Occasionally, Jessica would comment about losing her friends but her mother would sharply say, "You should just be glad your father provides so well for us. Any child would be grateful to have the luxuries you are given."

So Jessica kept her thoughts to herself. She was so lonely. While being an only child was tough in itself, being new in town with no friends made it much worse. Jessica winced as another pain shot up her arm. She felt so many emotions running through her right now. She wanted to cry. She wanted to be sad. Most of all, she wanted to be mad!

Jessica glanced up and saw her father standing in the doorway. "Hi princess, how are you?" Jessica's dad asked as he made his way to her bed. "Your mother told me what happened, honey. How on earth did you fall down the stairs?" Jessica looked impassively at her father and didn't utter a word. "Well, no matter princess, would you like me to bring your dinner up to you? Your mother made some spaghetti."

"No, thank you, daddy. I'm not hungry. I'm just very tired," Jessica replied.

"Okay, you go ahead and rest, Jessica. We'll come up and check on you later." Jessica's dad then rose from the bed and hastily left the room.

Jessica ran her fingers slowly up her cast then clenched her fist tightly as she seethed inwardly. She leaned back against the pillow, turned her face toward the wall, and choked back a sob. *Gosh, her arm hurt!* Sometime later in the night, Jessica felt someone's eyes piercing through her own sleepy ones. She cautiously raised one lid and discovered her mother staring at her. Jessica quickly closed her lid and feigned sleep. She opened both of her eyes when she heard her mother leave. She laid for a moment, unable to go back to sleep. While she was physically and emotionally exhausted, her mind just refused to let her rest. She closed her eyes once again and allowed her thoughts to wander. She roamed aimlessly for a while, thinking of nothing in particular. Suddenly, she realized she was in a house. A house not familiar to her at all.

Where was she? And why wasn't she afraid to be there? At that very moment, a man entered the room. He didn't frighten her at all. He moved slowly, deliberately. As he came closer, Jessica recognized him. It was Dr. LaMadrid. He had such a warm, loving expression on his face. Jessica instinctively moved closer to him. Dr. LaMadrid leaned down, picked Jessica up, then sat her down gently in a chair. Part of Jessica was skeptical because she knew she was experiencing something foreign to her. But, oh, it was so nice. She didn't want to even try to understand this. She put her arms around Dr. LaMadrid and snuggled deep into his neck. Jessica couldn't remember ever feeling this relaxed before. It was as if she knew this man, had always known him. She didn't know exactly why, but she knew she could trust him. And she knew, yes, she absolutely knew, that he would never let anything happen to her. And more importantly, he would never, ever do that to her, and he would be mad; he would be so mad if he knew someone had done that to her!

Jessica nestled deeper into the pillow that had become Dr. LaMadrid, exhaled slowly and faintly, and drifted off to sleep. It was the first time in a very long time that Jessica had fallen asleep with a trace of a smile on her lips.

CHAPTER THREE

LIFE WITH A CAST!

Jessica sat up abruptly in her bed and cried out. The pain in her arm was excruciating. Every part of her arm, from the tips of her fingers to her shoulder, ached fiercely. She closed her eyes for a moment and allowed the tears that had been controlled so carefully for so long, to escape. One by one, tears slid down her pale little cheeks, trailing slowly down her neck. Her lips tasted salty as the tears gushed forward now, seemingly endless. *WHY, WHY, WHY,* she thought, *why all this pain? Why did this horrible thing have to happen to me?*

She cautiously pulled a pillow from behind her and proceeded to remove the signs that would expose her innermost thoughts to anyone who might enter her room. She held the pillow warily against her face then moved it down her neck. Gosh, it was hard to do that with one hand. She wondered how she would ever manage to take a bath. *That will be difficult,* she decided. But she knew she would not ask for any help. That could only make things worse.

She eased her legs over the side of her bed and looked around her bedroom. Beautiful pink wallpaper with lovely flowers adorned her walls. Life-size stuffed animals in every corner. Her princess bed complete with all the right accessories. And her pictures of horses that were displayed proudly everywhere. Jessica loved horses! Her dad had promised her years ago that if they ever settled down for a longer period of time, he would buy her a horse. *"Oh, daddy, can I have an Appaloosa, please?"* While Jessica loved horses in general, the Appaloosa was her absolute favorite. Even though her father had answered yes to her having an Appaloosa, she had almost given up on the idea of having a horse at all. However, she was adamant of one thing - she would never stop loving them! As she glanced around the room again, she reflected; anyone who didn't know the truth would look around here and think I am the luckiest girl in the world.

Jessica stood up from her bed and for the first time realized that she had slept in her clothes. Then she became aware of how difficult it would be to do the simplest of things. It seemed to take forever to unbutton her blouse.

Her mother called to her from the bottom of the stairs, "Jessica, breakfast is ready."

"I'll be right down," Jessica yelled back.

"Do you need any help getting dressed?" her mom asked.

"Oh, uh, no, no, thank you. I'm almost ready," Jessica stammered. She quickly and painfully found something to put on. She slipped on some stretch shorts and after numerous attempts, found a blouse that would fit over her cast. Unfortunately, she still had to button it. After several tries, she was ready. She slipped her sling on, quickly ran a brush through her hair, and then left her bedroom.

She hesitated once again at the stairs but forced herself to go down, keeping her mind blank.

"You must be hungry, Jessica. You've not eaten a thing since lunch yesterday," her mother remarked.

"Yes, mother, I am hungry," Jessica softly answered.

As Jessica's mom made her breakfast, she mentioned casually, "You won't be going to school for the rest of the week. It's Thursday already and we'll go back to Dr. LaMadrid tomorrow. So, I'll be going a little later to get your homework from your teachers, okay?" Then she added, "Gee, we are really lucky, you know. It would have been much worse had your right arm been broken, since you are right-handed."

Jessica nodded slowly, almost choking on her food. She gently eased the cast down on the table as she continued to eat. She was really hungry. She ate both slices of the French toast her mother made, then downed 2 glasses of orange juice.

Well, she thought, *my arm still hurts, but at least my stomach feels better.* She excused herself from the table, then went into the family room. She wondered what she was missing at school today. Although she was very tired of moving, she felt lucky to be in school. She really liked her teachers and she was beginning to get to know some of her classmates. But at the moment, she was alone.

She watched some television for a while, then sat up stiffly in the chair as her mother approached. "I'll be right back. Jessica. I'm going to get homework from the school. Will you be okay until I get back?" Jessica's mother asked.

"I'll be fine, mother. I am just going to watch television, if that's okay," Jessica replied.

"Why, of course honey. That's perfectly fine!" her mom said. She walked over to Jessica and leaned down to kiss her cheek. Jessica didn't move a muscle. Long after her mother had gone, Jessica still felt the tautness in her body.

She was amazed at how cool and calm her mother was now. That left Jessica feeling worse actually. How could this nice mother be that way, too?! Everyone always told Jessica how nice and how beautiful her mother was. Jessica's mother had remarked once that the only reason she hadn't been able to make a career of modeling was because of her height. She was not quite tall enough.

Jessica's mom had beautiful blonde hair that just seemed to always look perfect. Each strand linked harmoniously to the next, all forming a gentle curve just past her shoulder blades. Jessica had heard her father mention how her mother's hair sparkled as though sprinkled with gold dust. She had her mother's hair color. She also had her eyes. It was difficult for Jessica to see how blue her eyes actually were when she looked in the mirror, but so many people would stop and stare at her and her mother, so she knew they had the same eye color.

Her mother was very beautiful and her father was the most handsome man she had ever seen. He had coal black hair that was naturally curly. Though Jessica's hair color came from her mother, her curls were from her father. Jessica's father had nice brown eyes also, but his most outstanding feature was his smile. He had beautiful white teeth and a smile that generated warmth. Jessica seldom saw him smile, though, and she wished he would do it more often. He was fine when it was just him and Jessica, but there was so much tension when her mother was there.

Sometimes, Jessica wondered what it would be like to be just with her dad. Somewhere deep inside, she felt her mother did love her; she just didn't understand. The phone ringing brought Jessica abruptly back to the present. "Hello," she answered.

"Hello, is this Jessica?" a voice on the other end asked.

"Yes, it is," she responded.

"Jessica, this is Karen from Dr. LaMadrid's office. He would like to see you tomorrow afternoon at 2:15 to check your cast. Do you think you can come?"

"Yes. I will tell my mother. We will be there at 2:15." Jessica said.

"Okay, we'll see you then. Bye, Jessica," Karen said.

"Bye, and thank you," Jessica finished.

When Jessica heard Dr. LaMadrid's name mentioned, her dream came flooding back. She was embarrassed. How could she face him? Would he know that she had dreamed about him? She leaned back in the chair and replayed the whole thing. Then she thought to herself, it will be alright, he is such a nice man. Though she dared not even think about it, somewhere in the back of her mind, she was anticipating seeing him again. Soon her mother returned bringing her work from school.

Jessica mentioned the phone call to her mother and listened as her mother called her father to discuss the appointment.

"I simply can't take her tomorrow. You know I have my hair appointment," her mother said harshly. There was silence for a moment. "Why can't you ever help me out? You always have an excuse! You can't take her to school, you can't help at home, and you don't have time for anything but your stupid work!" And with that, Jessica's mother slammed down the receiver.

Jessica didn't move. She was frightened. Her mother glanced at her and saw the unmistakable fear in her eyes. "Go and do your homework, Jessica. I will take you to your doctor's appointment tomorrow," she said sternly. She did as she was told.

Jessica slowly pulled the chair away from the dining room table. She was trying so hard to be quiet, but the chair moving over the wooden floor made it impossible.

Oh, if she just had the use of both her hands, she could pick the chair up. Finally, the chair was out far enough for Jessica to sit down. She did so soundlessly and then just waited for a moment. Silence. Jessica opened her history book and tried to concentrate on the Revolutionary War. She grew tired after a while and went in search of her mother.

"Mother," she said quietly. "I'm tired. May I take a nap?"

"Yes…and Jessica, we'll be having dinner alone tonight. Your father is leaving for northern California and he won't be back until next Friday," her mother said. Jessica's heart sank. She felt tears welling up again and left quickly for her bedroom. Jessica laid back on the bed and closed her eyes. She swallowed hard and fought the urge to cry. She wasn't sure if she wanted to cry because her dad was leaving or because her arm hurt. Probably both. She felt her eyes getting heavier until she finally fell asleep.

She awoke several hours later, feeling a little better. She wandered through the house and found her mother reading in the family room.

"Your dinner is in the oven. You had quite a long sleep," her mother said matter of factly.

Jessica ate her dinner, watched TV for a few minutes then went to her bedroom, undressed herself (which once again proved to be an ordeal), and searched for a nightgown that would slip over her cast. She laid in bed trying not to think about how much her arm still hurt. *Gosh,* she thought, *I hope I have enough nerve tomorrow to ask Dr. LaMadrid if it's supposed to hurt this much while it's getting better.*

CHAPTER FOUR

ALBERT GAINS SOME INSIGHT

Albert stared in the mirror and grimaced. He looked really tired. He was on call last night and had spent a good portion of it at the hospital. Fortunately, the cases were nothing too serious. A couple of kids with the flu, a possible appendicitis attack (which turned out to be negative), and one cut finger that required stitches. *This year,* he decided, *I definitely am taking a vacation.* If it materialized, it would be his first in over a dozen years.

He finished the last of his black coffee, kissed his wife, and then left for the office. When he arrived, as was his custom, he glanced at his appointments for the day. "Looks like we're in for another full day," he commented to his colleague, Dr. Lopez.

"Yes," Dr. Lopez said. "And I'm just about to begin, so I'll see you at lunch!" she quipped.

"You're probably right!" Albert laughed. That was a pretty common statement around the office. Although Albert, Dr. Lopez, and Dr. Goldberg shared the same office, they stayed so busy they might not speak again until lunch.

Before Albert knew it, it was already 12:20. "When is my next appointment, Karen?" Albert asked.

"At 1:30, Dr. LaMadrid. By the way, Jessica Ward will be in for a re-check at 2:15," Karen added.

Albert walked next door to Gino's, the Italian restaurant he had been frequenting for several years, and sat quietly in a corner by himself. He ordered spaghetti (it was the quickest) and was deep in thought when the waitress returned to his table.

"Would you like something to drink with your meal?" she asked.

"No, no, thank you," he replied hastily. He ate quickly, paid for his meal, then strode purposefully back to his office. He was anxious to see Jessica. He had the feeling that today would reveal more of Jessica's story. When he had finished his second patient of the afternoon, he glanced in the waiting room and saw Jessica seated beside her mother. She looked up at the same time and for a moment, they just looked at each other.

Albert waved to her and went to his next patient's room. This time, he was sure he saw fear on Jessica's face. He shook that off for a moment and listened intently as the patient's mother described what her baby boy had been experiencing. He checked the child over thoroughly, wrote out a prescription, and then prepared for his next patient, Jessica.

"Hello," he called as he entered Room 1. "Oh, hello, Dr. LaMadrid," Mrs. Ward responded.

"Well, let's see how we're doing today. Shall we, Jessica?" Dr. LaMadrid asked gently.

Jessica nodded uncomfortably. "Oh my goodness, I just remembered, I forgot to cancel my hair appointment! Doctor, may I borrow your phone for just a moment?" Mrs. Ward inquired.

"Sure. Just ask one of the receptionists," Dr. LaMadrid answered. That was interesting, he thought. He never allowed any of the patients or their families to use the telephone there.

He had, at one time, permitted it, but they tied up the phones, made long distance calls, and he heard inappropriate language more than once. This, however, was an exception. He needed an opening. When Mrs. Ward had left the room, he tried to break the ice. "You haven't lived here very long, have you, Jessica?" he asked.

"No," she whispered.

"Have you made any friends here yet?" he inquired as he checked her fingers for any signs of swelling.

"Not yet." her voice was barely audible.

He asked her other questions about her school and all were met with yes or no responses. Finally, he connected. "Do you have any hobbies?" he asked.

"I like horses," she said finding her voice. "No kidding! I ride all the time!" he was almost jubilant.

For reasons he didn't totally understand, it was terribly important to relate with this girl.

"Oh, do you have a horse of your very own?" she asked excitedly, her blue eyes as big as saucers.

"I sure do! But I keep her at a stable so she is fed and brushed properly. I just don't have the time for that," he answered.

Jessica looked at Dr. LaMadrid. She felt so comfortable with him. Out of the corner of her eye she saw her mother hang up the phone and thank the receptionist. She looked pleadingly at Dr. LaMadrid, touched his arm. She spoke so softly he had to lean over to hear, "Is my arm supposed to hurt this much to get well?"

He touched her fingers that protruded from her and prepared to answer when he felt her whole body become rigid.

"Thank you so much for letting me use your phone," Mrs. Ward said, "I would hate to lose my hair stylist. It takes so long to find a good one."

"No problem," Dr. LaMadrid answered. He continued to touch Jessica's fingers as he scrutinized her face. She had put her mask back on again. There was that impenetrable look again. "I think everything is going to be fine," he said to Mrs. Ward.

To Jessica, he said, "You know, when I was about your age, I broke my arm, too. For the first few days, it hurt so much! I was sure the doctor had made a mistake. But every day, it hurt a little bit less and then finally, it was all well." He winked at Jessica, turned to Mrs. Ward, and said, "I'll be back."

He left the room and came back a couple of minutes later with a sucker in one hand and a piece of paper in the other. "Can Jessica have this sucker?" he asked.

"Sure," Jessica's mom replied.

"Thank you," Jessica mumbled, not looking up.

"Oh, and by the way, here's the number and address of the stable where my horse is. Mrs. Ward, Jessica and I have a mutual interest in horses."

"If you have no objection, I would love to take her to the stable with me sometime. Of course, she couldn't ride right now, but sometimes I go and just brush her. I would really enjoy the company. I left my home phone number at the bottom. If you decide you would like to go, just give me a call. My wife and I have no children, and Suzanne, my wife, doesn't really enjoy going to the stable. You keep that in mind, won't you, Jessica?"

"I'm sure it would be fine for Jessica to go with you, and thank you for the invitation," Mrs. Ward sounded surprised but agreed.

Jessica took the paper Albert handed her and gazed into his eyes. She wanted to hug him. But, of course, she didn't. This time, when she said thank you, she looked at him and almost smiled. He patted her on the head, said good-bye, and left the room. He walked into his office and closed the door. That poor child, he thought. What had her mother done to make her so terrified of her? His suspicions were confirmed now-something was terribly wrong in that family!

But it also required delicate handling. Children, he knew, would instinctively protect their parents as a rule. Albert wanted very much to help her, but the first move has to come from her. He had, however, opened up a path for Jessica. He hoped she would decide to accept it. He was surprised at the way he reacted – first, to let Jessica's mom use his phone, then giving out his home telephone number. It was very rare for him to do that. But then, this was no ordinary situation either. This was Jessica. He suddenly felt weak all over.

He sat down on a chair for a moment and took a deep breath. He had seen some really ugly things throughout his medical career so he thought there was nothing that could affect him anymore. But right now, he felt different.

Jessica had moved him. He had done things that were totally out of character for him. Albert gulped down a small cup of water. He smashed the cup into a miniscule ball, tossed it into the trash, and after opening his office door, proceeded into Room 2, where an anxious parent looked beseechingly at him.

She spoke rapidly in Spanish while Albert listened intently. Her daughter, Marisa, had had a high fever all night and it hadn't dropped at all today. Albert, who was fluent in the language, spoke quietly and calmed the panicked mother as he examined the little girl.

Albert concentrated on the numerous other patients who continuously streamed in. When his last patient had gone, he glanced at his watch. It was 6:15! He raced to the phone and dialed his home. Suzanne answered on the first ring. "I'm sorry, I'm leaving the office right now," he said apologetically.

"Forget it Albert, we were expected at the Adamson's at 6:00," she answered with an exasperated sigh. "I called them already and let them know we couldn't make it."

"Gosh, I'm sorry, Suzanne. The time just got away from me. We could still go out to dinner, just the two of us. How does that sound?" he asked.

"Sure, that will be nice, I'll call Jeremy's and make reservations," she said. "Be careful, dear."

Albert left his office and arrived home shortly thereafter.

When they had been seated at their table for dinner, Albert filled Suzanne in on the events of the day. He gave Suzanne a detailed account of everything that had transpired between him and Jessica. When he was through, he asked Suzanne what her feelings were about Jessica and if she thought he had done the right thing.

"Yes, I think for the moment that's all you can do. She'll realize soon enough that you really want to help her," Suzanne answered.

Albert glanced at Suzanne's barely touched dinner and remarked, "Oh, I'm sorry. I didn't mean to spoil your dinner."

"Oh, no, you didn't. Actually, I'm not feeling too well. In fact, if you don't mind, I'd like to go home now." Suzanne said softly.

Albert quickly paid the bill and took his wife home. Suzanne seemed fine a little later, but Albert was concerned. Last week, she had felt nauseous and she looked pale.

He watched Suzanne sleeping soundly and felt a twinge of guilt. He definitely wanted to help Jessica but he would always keep his priorities straight. Albert rested his head on his pillow and stared at the ceiling. He turned off the light next to his side of the bed and laid down with a bemused look on his face. While Albert wasn't a religious fanatic, he maintained deep religious convictions. So his final thoughts that evening were comforting ones. He knew that God had a purpose for everything and when the time was right, it would be revealed to him.

Albert slept soundly that night but was awakened early by the sound of his wife retching in the bathroom. He was beside her in an instant. "Are you alright?" he asked worriedly.

"I think I have the flu," she answered weakly. Albert guided her back to their bed and after making her comfortable, he went to the kitchen to get her some water. Fortunately, today was Saturday. He checked quickly to make sure he wasn't on call.

He wasn't; it was Dr. Lopez who was on call today. He spent the morning taking care of Suzanne and around noon, she began to feel a little better. It was no wonder she was sick, Albert surmised. Suzanne was a teacher. She worked with children with special needs. It ran the gamut from those requiring little assistance to those needing a tremendous amount of guidance. It was a very taxing vocation but one that Suzanne was great at doing. It gave her a sense of helping people and a strong sense of accomplishment. But she was constantly coming down with something from the children. You would have thought the opposite would be true.

Albert was exposed regularly to every kind of contagious illness. He, however, seldom became sick. Just another affirmation from God that he was on the right course for his life, Albert thought. Later in the afternoon Suzanne commented, "I am going to make an appointment with Dr. Orren next week. I haven't felt well for a few weeks now. Last week, two of the children in the class were out with the flu, and the week before, four children had it.""

"Yes, I think that's a good idea," Albert agreed. "In fact, you should call early Monday. This being the flu season, Dr. Orren is probably very busy also."

Albert left the room then and went into the den. He wrote himself a reminder note that next week, on Thursday, April 20th, his wife would celebrate her 31st birthday. He would find just the right gift to lift her spirits. He wasn't sure what yet, but it had to be perfect!

CHAPTER FIVE

SO MUCH ANGER…
SO LITTLE ELSE

Jessica awoke on Saturday morning to the sound of pots and pans clattering. Then came the resonant voices that Jessica recognized as her parents'. From what she could hear, her father had shown up late last night and, while that should have made Jessica's mom happy, she was angry now because he needed to leave again right away. Her mother sounded furious. Jessica darted quickly under the covers and trembled violently. *I won't throw up, I won't throw up*, she repeated over and over in her head. She felt her tummy pushing hard up high in her chest; she tasted something terrible in her mouth. She threw back the blankets and made it to the bathroom without a second to spare. When the contents of her tummy had been emptied, she stood up and washed her face. Although the bathroom door was closed, she could still hear the muffled voices as they now began to escalate. Jessica tiptoed noiselessly back to bed and laid crossways as quietly as possible. Her parents could never have heard her with all the yelling going on downstairs. Jessica was consumed with fear.

These fights were always a precursor. Oh, she moaned inwardly. How come so soon? Usually, more time would pass between these episodes. She listened intently to the voices; she needed to know what had prompted this one.

"Jason, you never, ever stay home. I handle everything here! I have no friends, no life! Why are you doing this to me?" Jessica's mother shrieked.

"You know why Allison. How many times have we had this argument? You want money, don't you? Well, don' t you? It comes with a price, in case you have forgotten. I have to go where I am sent - it pays the best money, and you know that! Why do you keep throwing this in my face all the time?" Jason roared.

Jessica whimpered for a few moments then rose from the bed. There was nothing she could do now - she would just have to wait. She dressed herself, and this time, it took twice as long. The only thing worse than having to button her blouse with one hand was to have that hand shake so badly she needed to steady it with her cast.

She brushed her hair, then her teeth, and sat down on a chair. She tried to not listen to what was going on downstairs but it was very difficult. Before too long she heard the front door slam. She knew her father had left. *How could he leave me?* Jessica thought. She knew that he knew what he was leaving her open for. He didn't care about her either, she decided.

"Jessica," her mother's shrill voice interrupted her thoughts. "Get down here, NOW!"

No, I won't go, thought Jessica. But she was standing even as she was thinking this. Jessica had tried that approach before and it only made her mother angrier. Jessica braced herself and walked downstairs to where her mother was waiting, hands on hips and lips pursed. Looking directly at her mother, Jessica simply said, "Good morning, mother."

"Well, I guess it would be a good morning for me too if I could sleep all day long! I'm not your maid you know. Get in the kitchen and eat your breakfast before it gets colder!" Jessica's mother shouted.

"Yes mother," Jessica answered meekly. She knew it would not end there though. No, this was just the beginning. While the last thing Jessica's tummy wanted was food, she knew she had better eat. Cold eggs, dry toast, and warm milk. Jessica bit her lip to keep from crying.

Just as she raised her glass of milk to her lips, her mother yanked a handful of her hair from behind her. Jessica felt her neck snap as her mother said venomously, "Your hair looks terrible. I am going to make an appointment and have your hair cut off short. Maybe next time you'll take better care of it!" She relaxed her hold on Jessica's hair and for a moment, Jessica relaxed. *If it doesn't get any worse than this,* Jessica thought, *I will be alright.* She mopped up the spilled milk on the table with her napkin and patted her clothing quickly so her mother wouldn't see.

She cleared the table and was about to leave the room when her mother blocked her path. " You won't look so cute anymore when your pretty curls are all cut off, will you, Jessica?"

Jessica stood mute.

"Will you?" her mother was inches away from Jessica's face, looking menacingly at her.

"No, mother, I won't," Jessica spoke resignedly.

With an air of confidence and a twisted smile on her lips, her mother moved back. Jessica dared not take a breath. Her eyes remained glued to the floor, so she was totally unprepared as her mother's hand connected solidly with Jessica's tender face. Jessica's head reeled from the force of the blow. She struggled to maintain her balance. She desperately tried to focus on something. *Was her mother going to hit her again?* She glanced nervously around the room and discovered that her mother had left. Jessica waited. A long moment had passed and still her mother hadn't returned. Jessica walked back to her room.

She felt blood sliding down her chin. She could taste it in her mouth as well. She stood in front of her bedroom mirror and looked at her face. She took several tissues and wiped the blood off, only to have more appear. There was a nasty gash on her lower lip where her tooth had cut through. But even worse, there, on Jessica's face, in vivid color, were four complete indentations. Horrible marks left by the very woman who had brought her into this world. Jessica had been so sure that this last incident with her arm was the last. Her mother had wept uncontrollably when she realized the seriousness of the situation. She admitted that it was reprehensible for her to strike her child and vowed at that very moment that she would never raise a hand to her daughter again. *Not even a week had passed,* Jessica thought. She put some cool water on her face. It burned at the spot where she had been hit, but she continued to do it anyway. Her mother would be even angrier to discover a mark so clearly visible to anyone. Finally, after a few minutes, the blood on her lip stopped flowing.

Her lip was swollen badly and her cheek was puffy too. She turned the water off and attempted to pat her face dry. It hurt so much she put the towel down. She turned the television on and adjusted the volume a bit higher than usual. She laid down on her side and cried hysterically. *When is this going to end,* she asked herself. *Why does her father, who professes to love her so much, turn a deaf ear to this? Who will help me? Am I a bad girl? Do I deserve this?* She cried aloud.

Jessica started to fall asleep uncomfortably, fitfully, and painfully. She ached. But just as she closed her eyes, she panicked. *Oh, no, I shouldn't fall asleep this way! If mother sees me like this, she will be furious! I need to change my clothes.* But try as she might, her little body gave in to exhaustion and she drifted off. *Please God,* she begged, *don't let my mother see me like this!* She had always gotten up and changed before but this time, she just couldn't. No, this time, uncomfortable as she was, Jessica had fallen asleep. As the episodes worsened, so had Jessica's reactions. Poor little Jessica. On top of everything else, she had wet her pants.

CHAPTER SIX

SURVEYING THE DAMAGE

Jessica roused herself slowly from an emotional sleep. She felt absolutely drained. Every part of her body hurt. She slid gently out from under the pink flowered comforter and sat up. *My face must still be swollen,* she thought. It felt strange, like it belonged to someone else. Or perhaps she just wished that it did. She paused for a moment to collect her thoughts and then suddenly burst from her bed and into the bathroom. She quickly rinsed out her underwear and her shorts and after rolling them in a towel, hid them in her closet. She would remove them tomorrow when they were dry and put them in with the other laundry. After putting on some clean clothes, she went back into the bathroom, this time to check out her face. It was still swollen and marked still with her mother's fingerprints. *Gosh, it really stings,* Jessica thought. Jessica stood for a long moment at the mirror and watched as tears slid down past her eyelids. It made her lips hurt even more when the tears reached the open cut, but still she stood, immovable.

She let them flow unchecked and soon, the tears of sadness and despair became tears of anger and hatred. *Why doesn't she just kill me?* Jessica hissed into the mirror and added, *or why doesn't he?* One was just as guilty as the other, she determined. She wanted to walk down those stairs and confront her mother! But what could she say? And worse, what could she do when she was finished? She had no recourse whatsoever. Nowhere to go, no one to help her. *How unfair,* Jessica thought. *Anyone can have a child, do anything they want to that child, and that child is totally helpless!* It made her want to throw up again. *Why had they kept her if this was what they were going to do to her? No friends here, no family, no one to even talk to about this. Stop it!* Jessica said to herself. There was no point in thinking about it because it discouraged her even more. Physical pain, mental anguish; what a vicious circle. She walked away from the mirror and sat down at her desk in the corner of her room. She tried to smile as she looked at the horse pictures she had glued to the desktop.

Oh, her mom had gotten so mad. She pulled her blue notebook from a chair and put it on her desk. *Might as well try to study to take my mind off things,* she decided. When she opened the folder, there it was. She almost cried when she saw it. She picked up the paper and read each word carefully. *Jessica, If you ever want to go to the stables with me, please call Dr. Albert LaMadrid 555 4542.* Her hand trembled and she almost dropped the note. She couldn't; no, she just couldn't. He just wants someone to ride horses with. No, she certainly could not. Her parents would be livid! She put the note down and abruptly shut her notebook. But it was there, calling her, pleading for her to reach out, to ask for help. She stood up weakly and made herself look in the mirror again. She made her way back to her desk, took out the note, and moved silently into the hallway. You could almost feel the quiet just hanging in the air. Jessica's legs threatened to buckle underneath her. She heard her mother cough from downstairs and let out a sigh.

Now she could proceed. The hallway was dark even though it was 2:15 in the afternoon. She didn't turn on a light though. With a resolve she had no idea she had, she lifted the receiver. She felt sure her mother could hear her dialing; it sounded so loud. Fearfully, she finished pushing the numbers and it seemed barely a second had passed and it was ringing. Dr. LaMadrid answered on the second ring, "Hello." Pause. Silence. "Hello, is anyone there? Hello?" Jessica gently put the receiver down. Her mouth had opened but nothing would come out. She listened downstairs and heard her mother's voice calling her. Her stomach lurched. She picked up the phone again and dialed. Dr. LaMadrid answered again. "Hello? Hello?" Albert asked in an exasperated voice, "Is someone there?"

"I'm sorry," Jessica stammered. "I must have the wrong number." Jessica hung up the phone and walked downstairs to her mother, defeated.

CHAPTER SEVEN

PLAN A … AND PLAN B

Albert hung up the phone and returned to the living room. Suzanne immediately saw the puzzled look on his face and asked, "Who was that?"

"I'm not sure," Albert answered thoughtfully, then added, "I could have sworn that was Jessica's voice. That was the second call; the first time, no one spoke. The voice said she must have the wrong number. I'm almost positive that was her."

"Well, Albert, if it was Jessica," she spoke reassuringly, "she is trying to reach out for help. This is probably the early stage, so be patient until she gets a little stronger. I know how hard that will be for you." Suzanne glanced at her husband. He seemed so sad. For just a moment, she wanted to tell him about the possibility of her being pregnant. But what if she wasn't? It would make him feel worse. There had been other times when she felt like she was, but of course she hadn't been. This time though, she felt certain that she was. She had all the symptoms.

But she would wait to tell Albert when it was confirmed. She planned to take the test on Wednesday, then get the results on Thursday, her birthday. She hoped to have a birthday gift for Albert, too. This week just couldn't pass quickly enough for her!

Albert tossed and turned all night. He was sending Jessica telepathic messages. *Call me again, Jessica. It's all right. Let me help you. I am your friend. Call me, Jessica. Just call me.*

A few miles away, Jessica was also tossing and turning. All had been quiet throughout the evening. Her mother had avoided her completely. She went to bed early even though she wasn't really tired. It was safer that way. She stared up at the spotless white ceiling and thought about her options. Did she even have an option? She thought long and hard well into the night and eventually began to formulate a plan. *It probably won't work,* she thought bitterly. Then she added boldly, *It can't be any worse than what I'm going through right now.*

When Jessica returned home from school on Monday, she sat quietly at the table in the kitchen and proceeded to do her homework. Obviously, she had a lot to catch up on. And while she could write with her right hand, not having the use of her left hand made all her movements very uncoordinated. She immersed herself completely in her studies as her mother prepared dinner. Today, her mother was displaying a tremendous amount of contrition, which was customary for her. After a while, Jessica ventured to ask placidly, "Mother, do you know when daddy is coming home?"

"Next Saturday," her mother responded in a monotone voice.

Though no hint of an emotion crossed her face, Jessica 's mind was racing. That was too long, much too long. As Jessica grew older, instead of her mother becoming a bit softer, the opposite was true. Her mother was angrier; she hit much harder now, almost throwing caution to the wind. Yesterday was the first time her mother had left visible marks on her.

She ran her hand over her cast and touched her still swollen face. No, she wouldn't wait until Saturday. She would put Plan A into effect now.

Jessica and her mother ate dinner together that evening. Her mother had made macaroni and cheese and baby carrots. Those were two of Jessica's favorite foods. She ate light this evening, however. Her mother made small talk but for the most part, dinner was silent. It was so quiet at times that Jessica was sure her mother could hear her chewing her macaroni. She warily glanced at her mother and almost moaned out loud. Her beautiful mother. Jessica had been in love with her mother for as long as she could remember. She dimly recalled her mother dressing Jessica in her clothes, and putting on her some very expensive make-up. All except for the lipstick. Jessica's mother would apply it to her own lips first, then give Jessica a big kiss, and little Jessica would rush to the mirror to see her pretty red lips. It would always make Jessica giggle. Those times became fewer and fewer now though.

Jessica's mother seldom showed her any affection anymore. Oh, how she longed for someone to hold her and tell her they loved her! She stood up from the table and walked to the sink, balancing her plate, glass, and silverware precariously on her cast. She deposited them in the sink, then returned to remove her mother's setting. Her mother had left the room and Jessica heard the sound of the television playing in the family room.

Jessica finished her homework and waited patiently. Around 8 that evening, Jessica's mom called out, "I'm going up to take a bath."

"Okay mom," Jessica acknowledged. Jessica waited until she heard the bathroom door shut then she walked stealthily to the telephone. She dialed the number, then listened as the operator said, "Good evening, Patriot Inn. How may I help you?"

"Uh, Room 115, please," Jessica paused to clear her throat. "Room 115, please." Her voice was clearer now. "One moment. I'll connect you," the operator said.

The phone rang and rang. Jessica was just about to hang up when she heard a breathless, "Hello."

"Hi, daddy. It's me, " Jessica said softly."

"Hi, princess. Is everything okay?" her dad asked. Jessica almost never called her father when he was on the road.

"Well, mom's okay. But dad, I really need to talk to you about something," Jessica began.

"Oh honey, don't tell me you've found another horse you want," he said chuckling.

"No dad. I have to talk to you about something really important and I don't have much time," she answered firmly.

"What is it?" her dad seemed concerned.

"Daddy, I want you to come home and take care of me. And please," she continued, "Don't say anything until I finish. Daddy, I'm afraid to be with mommy. She hurts me, daddy. She gets so mad then she hits me, hard. Yesterday…" Jessica paused for moment, choked back a sob, then persevered. "Yesterday, daddy, she pulled my hair. Then she smacked my face so hard she left her fingerprints, and I bit my lip, and, and… Daddy, I don't care what mommy told you. She pushed me down the stairs and that's how my arm got broken. Please, please, daddy, come and get me, daddy. Please."

Tears flowed now from Jessica's eyes but she held her breath, waiting to hear her father's response.

"Now, Jessica," he spoke haltingly. "Don't you think you're over-reacting a little bit? I know your mother has a terrible temper but really, honey, you know your mother would never purposefully push you down the stairs. I know you're lonely and you're hurting, but so is your mother. Be patient with her. Okay, princess? She really loves you. You will make some friends soon then everything will be fine. Really."

For a moment, Jessica was stunned. This was not at all the reaction she had expected. No, she hadn't planned on this. She had expected her dad to drop the phone, grab the first plane out of Sacramento, and come and get her.

She felt an indescribable loss at that moment. She knew that somewhere inside, her dad knew that she was telling the truth. Why wouldn't he just say it? It was so much easier not to have to deal with it. Maybe it would go away.

"Bye, daddy," Jessica whispered then hung up the phone.

"Good night, princess. I love you," she heard him say as she rested the receiver back into its natural position. Jessica went up to her room and undressed quickly. She had brushed her teeth and climbed into bed when she heard her mother leaving the bathroom. She closed her eyes to fake being asleep but she needn't have bothered. Her mother didn't even glance in her direction but made her way back downstairs and sat down in front of the television. Jessica remained undaunted. She really didn't understand why though. Her dad's uncaring attitude should have devastated her. And it really had hurt her.

But the one thing Jessica had always been was tenacious. She wouldn't quit now-not now. She turned her tired little face on the pillow and closed her eyes, only allowing a few tears to escape. Her mind struggled to find a pleasant thought. Suddenly, she was back in that room. And there he was again. Without a moment's hesitation, she climbed up on his lap and put her arms around his neck. Albert rocked her back and forth gently as he wiped away her tears. Soon Jessica fell fast asleep. She slept soundly throughout the night, occasionally tightening her grip on her pillow as she rocked silently back and forth.

CHAPTER EIGHT

ALBERT GETS INVOLVED

Jessica put her books in her pretty pink backpack then prepared to leave for school. She woke up late this morning so she was in a rush. No time even for breakfast. "Mom," she called out. "Shall I walk to school or are you going to drive me?"

"It's your own fault you're late, young lady. You should walk!" her mother shouted from the next room.

Jessica shut the door behind her and almost ran the three and a half blocks distance to the Viewmont Elementary School. The first bell was just ringing when she got there. She had exactly four minutes to get into her seat. She made it, but barely. Tamara, the girl who sat beside her, smiled and they both giggled a little bit. Jessica liked Tamara. She had short dark brown hair that hung straight just below her ears, lively brown eyes, and a real nice smile. Jessica had only spoken to her a few times but she hoped to get to know her better.

Jessica's teacher, Mrs. Garcia, began the school day as she always did, with math, then English. Jessica liked Mrs. Garcia, too. She was short, a little plump, and just really seemed to enjoy her life - something Jessica very much admired. Soon, it was time for lunch. Jessica had her lunch tray balanced carefully, half on her cast, and half with her right hand. As she found a seat and placed her tray on the table, she saw Tamara coming up beside her.

"Can I sit here with you?" Tamara asked.

"Sure," Jessica answered pleasantly. Soon the girls were eating and chatting. "What happened to your arm?" Tamara inquired.

"Well," Jessica stammered. "I, uh, fell down the stairs in my house."

"Wow, that must have really hurt!" Tamara remarked then added, "You probably just hadn't gotten used to your new home yet, right?"

"Yes, you are probably right, " Jessica said uncomfortably.

"Hey, when you get your cast off, do you want to go roller skating? I go every Friday night, almost. My parents take me at 7:00 then pick me up at 9:00. It's really great - all the kids from school go and the music is so cool! Oh gosh. I almost forgot, you do skate, don't you?" Tamara finished.

"Well, I skate, but I'm not very good," Jessica replied.

"That's okay. Don't worry, you'll get a little better every time you go. You should have seen me a year ago, I could barely stand up!" Tamara giggled.

Jessica laughed, too, and they set a tentative skating date for the Friday following the removal of her cast. Jessica felt pretty good right now. She had begun to cultivate a friendship. They walked back to class together, talking and chuckling all the way. The remainder of the school day flowed very nicely for Jessica. She had caught up on all her schoolwork and her class was just beginning a new project. The entire third grade class would be putting on a play for Cinco de Mayo!

Mrs. Garcia explained that Cinco de Mayo was the Mexican celebration of the defeat of the French army on Mexican land. Mrs. Garcia was in charge of the play, and tomorrow there would be an actual audition to find out who would play which part. Jessica knew she couldn't do too much with her cast but she was excited about it anyway.

Mrs. Garcia walked over to Jessica and whispered to her that she had a very special part for her to play! Everything was great, until the bell rang, signaling the end of the school day. She said good-bye to her new friend Tamara, who rode the bus, then gloomily walked home. When she opened the front door, she encountered her mother on her way out. Jessica's mother was in a terrible mood, and Jessica felt relieved that she was leaving.

"I'm going to meet my friend, Lisa, for a while, then do some shopping. I'll be home later," her mother said. "Make yourself a sand-wich for dinner." And with that she slammed the door and was gone.

Jessica pulled out a chair in the kitchen and sat down. She had no reservations about what she was going to do. She did not deserve this, she knew that. She pushed herself away from the table and found the number. This time, when she heard the phone ringing, she was calm. Well, sort of. When the pleasant voice on the other end answered, she knew exactly what she was going to say.

"Good afternoon, Dr. LaMadrid's office."

"Hello. May I please speak to Dr. La Madrid?" Jessica asked.

"Who's calling, please?" the receptionist asked.

"This is Jessica Ward," she stated.

"Dr. LaMadrid is with a patient right now, He may need to call you back; can you hold on for a moment?"

Oh no, thought Jessica, *she hadn't anticipated that! What if he called later and her mother was home?* She was seriously considering hanging up when she heard Dr. LaMadrid saying, "Hi Jessica, how are you? Are you having a problem with your arm?"

"No, no, I'm okay," she said softly. *He is so nice,* she thought. Then she quickly asked, "Are you busy?"

Albert looked at the filled examining rooms and the waiting room teeming with patients then answered, "No, not at all. What can I do for you, Jessica?"

"Uh, well, I was wondering if I could go to the stable with you sometime?" she asked hesitantly then added, "But I know how busy you are and it wouldn't have to be right away."

Albert couldn't believe what he had heard, but he needed to repress some of his excitement. "Hey, that's a great idea! Really, Jessica, I need to go, I haven't been there for quite a while. Let me just check my schedule - hold on," Albert said. He put her on hold then looked swiftly at his schedule for the next few days. A moment later, he was back. "How about Friday afternoon, after I finish, maybe around 4:30? How does that sound?" Albert asked cautiously.

Albert hoped that this week would pass quickly and uneventfully for little Jessica. He told Suzanne about the call from Jessica when he arrived home that evening. He had mixed emotions when he told his wife. He was happy that Jessica had called, sad that this was happening to her, but more than anything, he was afraid for her.

"You know, Albert, that probably was Jessica who called the other day. She knows you want to help her and pretty soon, she is going to let you. When do I get to meet her, anyway?" Suzanne asked.

"That is top priority, believe me. You are going to love her. I just know it," he said while hugging her. Later, Suzanne noticed that for the first time in quite a while, her husband was sleeping peacefully. *Albert will help that little girl, and I will too,* she thought. Then she grinned to herself. Tomorrow was her pregnancy test. She almost giggled out loud. She was confident now that the test would be positive. This morning, she couldn't fit into a pair of her pants! She was glad she had waited a few months. Albert would be absolutely thrilled!

Allison Ward entered her home that evening angry at the whole world. She had met with her friend, Lisa, hoping to relieve some of her stress. But it had just upset her more. Lisa's life seemed perfect next to her own. She knew it wasn't, but right now she wasn't being rational. Lisa's husband worked here in town, made great money, and helped Lisa with her two children. Everything Allison's husband did not have or do.

While Jason made good money also, for Allison, it just wasn't worth it. It never really had been. Years ago, she had asked Jason to stay in one place and take a cut in his pay. But he was so sure that his way was the best way. After a while, Allison had accepted it and now depended on that extra money. But a rage consumed her inside. A rage that channeled outwardly in only one direction - toward her daughter. Allison felt that it was only in that area where she had any kind of control over anything. She moved every time Jason said, to every place Jason said, and spent money the way Jason said. Just the thought of it made her furious!

She slammed doors and threw things then turned abruptly to see Jessica standing there. Allison wanted to vent her hatred on her. She shouldn't have it so easy. It was a tough, cold world out there;

she might as well find out about it now. She looked at Jessica and saw absolute terror in her eyes. For a second, she didn't care. Finally, she shoved Jessica toward the stairs and said gruffly, "Get up to your room…NOW!"

Jessica fled up the stairs, taking two steps at a time. She cowered behind her bedroom door until she was sure it was safe.

Jessica wasn't sure whether she slept that night or not. Wednesday morning, when Jessica's mother was feeling guilty about her behavior the night before, Jessica asked meekly, "Mother, may I please go to the horse stable with Dr. LaMadrid on Friday afternoon?"

"Did you call him or did he call you?" she asked.

"He called me," she lied. "He said he needs to go because he hadn't gone there for a long time. Please," Jessica begged. "I can't ride but Dr. LaMadrid said I could help brush her. He also said he will pick me up," she added.

Well, Allison thought to herself, *Jason will be out of town, and it would give me an opportunity to go out.* "I suppose so," she said, quite irritated.

Jessica held everything in until she was alone. "Yes, yes, yes!" she exclaimed with delight. Finally, a victory! Granted, a small one, but a victory nonetheless. She was practically jubilant all day at school and she raced home immediately after. She called out a greeting to her mother, who mumbled something from upstairs, then raced to the phone. She knew the number by heart. "Hello, this is Jessica Ward. May I please speak to Dr. LaMadrid?"

"Hold on just a moment please," the receptionist answered.

"Hello Jessica, how are you?" Albert asked.

"I'm okay, thank you. And you?" she inquired.

Albert smiled. She was mannerly as well. He wasn't surprised. "I'm well, thank you. I hope you have some good news for me," he stated cautiously.

"I'm so happy," Jessica gushed. "My mom says I can go on Friday. But do you think you could pick me up?"

"Of course, I'd be glad to," Albert responded.

"Are you sure, doctor? I don't want you to go to any trouble?" she asked softly.

"Nonsense, we have a date for Friday afternoon at 4:30. Now, tell me how to get to your house," he finished.

Jessica gave him directions then they said their farewells. "Jessica, I hope you know that I am really looking forward to this," Albert's voice showed emotion.

"I am, too," Jessica's voice cracked. "Thank you, Dr. LaMadrid. I'll see you Friday. Bye."

Albert told Suzanne about Friday afternoon and invited her to come.

"No," she begged off. "But you will bring her by here for some hot chocolate, won't you?"

"I sure will. You make the best hot chocolate, Suzanne! She is just going to love you, I tell you!" Albert said lovingly as he embraced his wife.

"By the way, what did the doctor say?" Suzanne caught herself just in the nick of time. She wouldn't tell Albert until they called with her test results. Tomorrow night she would tell him, over her birthday dinner. *Ugh,* she thought. *Just the thought of food made her feel sick.*

"Well, he said to take it easy. Probably just the flu." Suzanne had to look away while she spoke. The temptation to tell him right now was so great.

Wednesday evening passed quietly for Jessica. Her father had called and spoke to her for a while. He wanted to get her a new bike and new skates on Saturday when he came home. Jessica listened until he was through then thanked him politely. He had become like a stranger to her now. She went to bed and took down her alarm clock. It was 8:30. She did some fast figuring in her head. Only 44 more hours and she would be with Dr. La Madrid. She couldn't wait!

Dr. La Madrid sailed through his work load on Thursday. He had gone at noon and picked up the birthday gift for his wife. He remembered a few days ago that sometime back, while they were out shopping, Suzanne had picked up this musical clown (she had an affinity for clowns). She had put it back down though when she saw the price. *Suzanne will be surprised,* Albert thought.

He had no idea what was in store for him. He would be the one to be surprised tonight!

He walked in his front door, birthday gift in hand, promptly at 5:00 PM. Dinner reservations at 6:00; time enough for a quick shower, and then into his suit. Suzanne, however, was nowhere to be found. He proceeded to get ready and at about 5:25, Suzanne breezed in.

"Sorry I'm late. I just wanted to get something new for tonight," she said, chuckling under her breath. She had 4 bags in her hand that she hid in the closet. *He could see those later,* she decided. She never imagined it would be such fun shopping for maternity clothes!

"Suzanne, you look absolutely beautiful," Albert remarked. She just seemed to glow, he noticed. "I can see that birthdays agree with you!"

"Thank you, and you look very nice, too," she said while giving him a kiss.

They arrived at the restaurant right on time. The maître d seated them at a lovely table with a view of the ocean. After ordering their food, Albert produced his gift for his wife. She read the card first, visibly touched by Albert's selection. Then she opened her present. She was genuinely surprised. "I can't believe it! I didn't even know you saw me looking at it," she said demurely.

"Are you kidding?" he joked. "I know everything you do!"

"My sweet husband," Suzanne began shyly. "Not everything. I have a little surprise, or shall I say, gift for you!"

Now it was Albert's turn to be surprised. He looked at Suzanne. Was she blushing? "Well, what is it?" he asked excitedly.

"I wanted to tell you sooner, but I needed to wait until I was absolutely positive, and now I am." She paused for a little dramatic effect. "We are going to have a baby, Albert dear! Isn't that wonderful?" Suzanne spoke softly and lovingly.

"Oh, my gosh, Suzanne! I can't believe it! Are you sure? Did you have a test; when-" he stopped in mid-sentence, rose from his chair, and kissed his wife delicately on the cheek. "I love you, Suzanne," he murmured sweetly. His eyes filled with tears and so did Suzanne's.

For a moment, they said nothing but just allowed this wonderful moment to wash over them. It was the first time Suzanne had spoken the words aloud, and it had hit her, too. A baby! For them! From God! Life was beautiful! Neither Albert nor Suzanne ate much of their dinners. Albert, because he was excited, thrilled, elated; and Suzanne, because she was all those things - and nauseous, too! Albert made a fuss over Suzanne that night and insisted she cut back on her work schedule. "Don't worry," she agreed. "I don't feel up to those long days right now."

With that, she curled up on the bed and was asleep exactly a minute after. Albert tucked her in then climbed in next to her. What an incredible day! He said a prayer thanking God for this great gift. The doctor told Suzanne that the baby was due sometime in late October. She had been let down so many times before that. This time, she waited 3 whole months.

Wow, thought Albert, *I'm going to be a daddy!* He pondered that for a moment and thought of all the things it encompassed. He was almost asleep when Jessica's face flashed in front of him. Tomorrow, he would take her to the stable. He could only hope that it would open up another door. While he always had faith, after tonight, he just knew everything would work out. How, he didn't know, he just knew it would.

CHAPTER NINE

THE STABLE

Friday afternoon, Jessica arrived home from school to find her mother glaring at her in the doorway. *She was obviously in one of her moods,* thought Jessica.

"Hurry up and get in here," her mother snapped.

Jessica rushed into the kitchen and turned to face her mother.

"Well, if you're going to go with Dr. LaMadrid, you had better move. And you are not going in those clothes!" Jessica's mother said sarcastically. She then followed Jessica upstairs and into her bedroom. Jessica pulled some jeans out of her closet and was about to reach for her sweatshirt when her mother pushed her aside demanding, "What is that towel doing in here? And it's wet, too! I want you to tell me what happened right NOW!"

"I, I, I spilled some juice on my clothes and I didn't want you to get mad at me, so I washed them out myself. I'm sorry, mother," Jessica said apologetically.

Jessica's mother looked like she was going to hit her and Jessica braced herself for the blow. But instead, her mother grabbed Jessica's good arm and shook it. Hard. So hard, in fact, that Jessica felt her teeth rattling. Then she pushed her, and Jessica fell backwards across her bed. "Get dressed and get downstairs! If you're not ready in 5 minutes, you're not going!" Jessica's mother left the room fuming.

Jessica had no time to check for physical damage, so she dressed quickly and neatly. She brushed her hair, her teeth, then took the wet towel with her and left the room. She laid her clothing out on the washing machine to dry. *That will probably make her mad, too,* thought Jessica. But she didn't know what else to do. Jessica's mother hated her, Jessica couldn't deny that anymore. Time had only made it worse. Jessica felt a deep fear inside her. A fear that no matter how hard she tried to sweep aside, continued to grow and become more and more real. Jessica feared for her life!

Albert showed up promptly at 4:30. He walked to the door and rang the bell. Allison Ward opened the front door and invited Albert inside. *What a lovely home,* thought Albert. He glanced around the room trying to look without appearing to be prying. After the greetings had been issued, Jessica entered from the kitchen. "Hi, Jessica," Albert called. "Are you ready to go?"

"Yes, thank you, doctor. I'm ready," Jessica answered timidly. "Mrs. Ward, if you have no objections, I'd like to take Jessica to my home to meet my wife. We will have her back home by 8:00, if that's okay?" Albert finished.

"Sure, that's no problem. Just have fun," Jessica's mom said. She leaned to kiss Jessica and again, Albert noticed Jessica's panicked look that fled as quickly as it had come. "Be a good girl, Jessica. And have a good time!" Jessica's mother called after them.

Albert opened the passenger door and after Jessica climbed in, he fastened her seat belt. She seemed kind of distant, almost aloof. *Maybe she's shy,* he reasoned. They made small talk all the way to the stable. Jessica told him about her role in the Cinco De Mayo play. Mrs. Garcia had selected her to be the narrator. "Would you teach me a few words in Spanish?" she asked meekly.

"Yes, I'll be glad to," Albert said then added, "I mean, *si, "con mucho gusto!"* They shared a laugh together.

With every mile that passed the tension became less and less. *That was a good sign,* Albert noted. Soon, they arrived at the stable. Jessica couldn't believe it; there were horses everywhere! Black, brown, white, all kinds of colors and mixtures, just the most incredibly beautiful horses! Albert noticed this and remarked, "You know, I hope you'll want to come here often. I would love the help, and especially the company."

"Gee, I'd love to!" Jessica answered exuberantly.

Albert took her by the hand and guided her toward his horse. Jessica glanced quickly and knew it was his horse. She squealed and ran in that direction. Suddenly, she stopped and turned toward Albert. *Maybe he would be mad,* she thought. *But no, he was actually laughing - it was perfectly okay.* "Oh, she's so beautiful. What's her name?" Jessica asked.

"Her name is Athena. Have you studied anything in school about Greek mythology yet?" he asked.

"No, not yet," she seemed puzzled.

"Well, Athena was the goddess of wisdom and the arts," Albert continued talking about Athena, and Zeus, the king of the gods. He told her the story of how he had always wanted a horse and how his parents could never afford to give him one. So, now he had his horse, but he wanted to make sure she received the best possible care. That was why he kept her here. Jessica knew she had never seen a more beautiful horse.

She gently stroked Athena with her right hand and she was sure that Athena was enjoying it. Athena was dark brown, with a few white patches between her eyes. Jessica loved it here with Dr. LaMadrid. She wished she could stay here forever.

Albert moved next to her then commented, "Wait until you ride her, Jessica. It's like nothing you have ever felt before!"

Jessica tried so hard not to cry but it was all to no avail. A few tears had escaped and were sliding slowly down her cheeks. He was so nice, why couldn't he be her daddy? She turned away so Dr. LaMadrid wouldn't notice, but it was too late.

"What's the matter, Jessica?" Albert asked.

"Nothing. Really, I'm fine," she replied.

He turned her toward him and asked directly, "Why are you crying?"

"I'm so sorry. Please forgive me. I think I should go home," she cried.

"No, please, Jessica," Albert sounded distraught. Then he just couldn't stop himself. "I know something is wrong, Jessica. Though I don't know you that well and you don't really know me either. I know you're hurting, and I want to help you. Really, I do. You can trust me, Jessica. I am your friend. Please let me, please."

Albert guided Jessica away from the stable and knelt down. Jessica's little body was racked with sobs as she looked at Albert and begged, "Please don't let my mommy hit me anymore." With one sweep, Jessica was in Albert's arms and she let go of all the terrible things pent up inside her. Albert was struggling to maintain his composure. Finally, the words had been spoken. Now he could help her. He bit his lip hard to keep from crying then asked Jesssica if it was alright to take her to his home. She just nodded to say yes.

Albert strapped her in, took a tissue, and cleaned her face. Then he said softly, "Everything is going to be okay now. You can believe me." He climbed into the driver's seat and they left the stable.

Jessica was feeling so many things - she was embarrassed and shy, but more than anything, she was afraid. What had she done? It seemed to take just a minute to get to Dr. LaMadrid's home.

"You're going to love Suzanne," he said. "She's so excited to meet you." Albert saw the apprehension in her eyes, walked to her side of the car, and took her hand as they walked up the drive.

"Hi," Suzanne greeted as she opened the front door. "You're early. I don't have the hot chocolate ready yet."

"Jessica, this is my wife, Suzanne. Suzanne, this is Jessica." Albert made the introductions brief. Jessica stood in the living room and didn't move. She couldn't move. She couldn't speak either. She couldn't believe it.

This was the room from her dream! And there, over in the corner, was the chair Dr. LaMadrid had rocked her in! Jessica was overwhelmed. Suzanne gave Jessica a hug (which caused her to flinch for a moment), then they all sat down together.

Albert was shaken also. He told Suzanne what Jessica had told him. Jessica sat quietly and waited. *Maybe Suzanne would be mad at her,* Jessica thought. Instead, Suzanne rushed over beside her and put her arm around her. That felt so nice to Jessica.

Albert sat on the other side and slowly, Jessica's story unfolded. She told them everything, from the time when she was two or three until what happened before Albert picked her up. Albert and Suzanne were incensed. It hit them perhaps even a bit harder after the long wait they had endured just to have an opportunity to become parents. Before Jessica finished, all three were crying. After a while, Suzanne looked at Albert and winked, saying, "I think we should make some hot chocolate now. Why don't you make a few phone calls and we'll go get it ready?"

"Sounds great! Jessica, do you feel like a nice cup of hot chocolate?

"If you're sure it's no trouble," she answered politely.

"Oh," Suzanne said, "you are so sweet. Come on honey, let's go into the kitchen." She took Jessica's hand and together, they got all the ingredients ready to make the hot chocolate. It was a nice diversion for Jessica, who had absolutely no idea of what was in store for her. She only knew how very good she felt at that moment.

Even better at the next one when Suzanne mentioned, "You had better watch me carefully this time, because pretty soon I'll ask you to make it yourself. We are going to have a baby in October and I just may not feel up to doing it!"

"Congratulations!" Jessica said warmly then she added shyly, "My birthday is in October, too."

"Really, what day?" Suzanne asked. "My birthday is on the nineteenth. Um, does Dr. LaMadrid like whipped cream or marshmallows on his hot chocolate?" Jessica questioned.

"That silly guy likes them both," Suzanne laughed. "Now, you know Jessica, you simply cannot refer to him as Dr. LaMadrid. So you think about what you would like to call him."

Remembering the story Albert had told her at the stable, Jessica stated emphatically, "I already know what I will call him. I will call him Zeus!" Suzanne smiled as Albert entered the kitchen and she whispered to Jessica, "I'll call him my Zeus, too."

CHAPTER TEN

NOW WHAT?

Albert looked solemnly at Jessica as they drank their hot chocolate. "Jessica," he began slowly. "We need to talk about how we're going to handle this problem. Do you have any other family living near here that you know of?"

"I have an uncle who lives in Florida. He's my dad's brother. I see him occasionally at Christmas. My mother has one sister and one brother, but she hasn't talked to them for several years," she replied.

"How about friends?" Suzanne asked.

Jessica looked ready to cry again. "My mother has lots of friends but when they find out that I talked to you, they will be really mad."

Suzanne looked pleadingly at Albert. "Did you talk with anyone who might be able to help us?"

"Well, I called Tom and he said he'll drop by a little later." He looked at Jessica and said, "Tom is our good friend, and he is also a police sergeant. Do you trust Suzanne and I, Jessica?"

"Yes," she whispered, looking straight at him.

"We want you to stay here with us tonight." He saw the fear in her eyes, but he continued, "Honey, you know your mother is getting worse, and Suzanne and I are afraid for you to go back there. You said you tried to talk to your father but he rejected you. I know that your father is aware of what your mother is doing to you, but he just chooses to ignore it. But Suzanne and I won't-we can't!"

Jessica was sobbing now, "She'll kill me when she's alone with me again."

"No, she won't, because until she gets help for her problem, we won't let her be alone with you!" Albert and Suzanne were both speaking now. "It's hard for you to understand, Jessica, but your mother is sick. Not sick physically, but she needs to talk to someone about her anger. It's not right and she needs help first so she never hurts you again. It's good for herself as well."

"But I don't have any clean clothes or my toothbrush, " she said in a low voice.

Ernie, Albert's dog, picked that moment to make his appearance. He sniffed Jessica for a moment then licked her arm. Albert said, "Oh, he likes you Jessica!" Ernie won't usually go around people he hasn't seen before. "By the way, his name is Ernie."

Ernie proceeded to put his head directly on Jessica's lap, and Jessica began to pet him gently.

"We know that for a very long time, you have shouldered a lot of responsibilities. For anyone really, but for a seven-year-old, you have done remarkably well. But Suzanne and I want to take care of you. For tonight, don't worry about a thing. Everything is going to be fine, and you know I tell you the truth. It's difficult I know, but just trust us." With that, Albert picked Jessica up out of her chair and carried her into the living room, with Ernie at his heels. He sat down in the rocker (her dream chair) and slowly rocked her back and forth. *She shouldn't relax,* she thought, *shouldn't fall asleep.*

There was so much to think about. But oh, this felt so good! She felt all the tension leaving her body. It really was just like her dream, she thought. *No,* she decided, *this was much, much, better.*

Suzanne tiptoed in a few minutes later and all was quiet, except for the gentle snoring coming from Jessica. *Gosh,* Suzanne thought, *not even 5 minutes had passed.* Jessica was physically and emotionally drained. Suzanne followed closely behind Albert as he carried Jessica to their guest room. She pulled back the blanket as Albert tenderly laid her down. Together, they covered her and stood staring for a moment.

"Poor little angel," Albert said softly. "We are in this with her now. No one is going to hurt her again, " Suzanne said resolutely. They walked back into the living room just as their friend Tom pulled up. He moved quickly up the drive as Albert greeted him anxiously. Together, Albert and Suzanne filled him in on everything they knew.

"I hope you don't mind but I invited someone else over. Her name is Renee, and she is with the Protective Child Services. She can tell us what to do next, " Tom said.

"Should I call Mrs. Ward and tell her Jessica isn't coming home tonight?" Albert asked.

"Let's just wait. Renee will be here soon," Tom answered. Albert quietly took Tom into the bedroom and showed him Jessica. Albert noticed how peacefully she slept, even with her cast. Tom went back into the living room and Albert joined Suzanne in the kitchen. She was making some coffee.

Albert walked up to her and embraced her while asking, "How are you feeling, sweetheart?"

"Oh, I'm okay. A bit tired, but Albert, we just have to talk the Protective Child Services people into letting Jessica stay here with us. I can't bear the thought of her staying somewhere with complete strangers," Suzanne said with determination. *How ironic,* she thought, *I just met her a few hours ago myself.*

"I know," he said quietly. "I just knew you would feel the same way I do. Come on, I'll finish the coffee – and you are going to sit down!"

"Yes sir," she laughed, but she did go in and sit down. She was tired. It felt so good to pick her feet up.

When the doorbell rang a moment later, Tom jumped up to answer it. "Hi, Renee. Thanks for coming out this late. This is Albert and Suzanne LaMadrid." Tom quickly made the introductions. They all sat down and once again, Albert repeated what he knew about Jessica Ward.

"Poor child," Renee commented. "How about the father. Is he any help at all?"

"No. In desperation, Jessica begged him to come and get her and she actually stated that her mother had pushed her down the stairs. He ignored her plea completely, appearing as though she had contrived the whole thing." Albert felt the anger rise in him again.

"Any other family around this area that you know of?" Renee asked.

"No, Jessica spoke as though there were no other family members close, or even good family friends." Albert responded. He bent slightly in his chair and looked intently at Renee.

"Please," he began. "You have to let Jessica stay here with us. I know that, as a rule, children like her are put in a foster home until their fate has been decided, but Jessica is so vulnerable right now. She needs Suzanne and I, and we need her, too."

"Oh, Albert, I don't know. It would be very unusual. I will need to talk with a few people to check on the feasibility. Believe me, I'll do everything in my power to keep her here. Just knowing that after everything she's been through, she's sleeping soundly in your room tells me so much." Renee had taken a peek at her, too, when she first arrived. "We will certainly keep her here tonight, and tomorrow we will get things rolling.

Standing up, Renee said, "Tom and I will stop by and let Mrs. Ward know that Jessica has been taken into protective custody. She need not know that Jessica is here. If she calls or attempts to create any problem at all, notify Tom and myself right away." She handed Albert her card, then stopped at the door once again to say directly to Albert and Suzanne, "Ordinarily, Jessica's case would be turned over to a case worker. I rarely do it anymore but this time, I will handle Jessica's case myself. We'll all do our very best. Goodnight."

"Thank you, Renee." As he firmly shook Tom's hand, Albert said emotionally, "Thanks, buddy. I can't tell you how much we appreciate this."

Tom winked at Suzanne and remarked, "Don't worry, I plan on getting at least one of Suzanne's great Italian dinners out of this!"

"You got it," Suzanne laughed. "And soon, too!"

With that, Tom and Renee left. Albert and Suzanne stood in the living room for a few moments, then decided they had better get some rest.

They both offered up a prayer, asking that Jessica be allowed to stay with them, at least for now. They fell asleep holding hands, both fighting the urge to bring Jessica in with them. Would she awaken in the night and be afraid in a strange bed? Would she call for them if she did? Well, it wasn't long before they had the answers. Albert wasn't sure exactly what time of the night it was when Jessica tiptoed into their bedroom. She brought her blanket and pillow and laid down on the floor next to where Suzanne was sleeping. Ernie followed right behind and he laid right next to Jessica. Albert squeezed Suzanne's hand and she squeezed back. Now they could sleep. *Should I get up and turn off the hallway light that Jessica had turned on?* Albert thought. *No, this picture was perfect - it would stay that way for tonight.*

CHAPTER ELEVEN

ALLSION CONFRONTED

Allison jumped when she heard the doorbell. Jessica was three hours late - she was in big trouble. Allison was furious when she yanked open the front door. She was caught totally off guard to see Tom and Renee standing there.

"Mrs. Ward?" Renee asked.

"Yes, that's me. Who are you?" she demanded.

"I am Renee Benoit, and this is Sergeant Tom O'Donnell of the Fountain Police. I work for the Protective Child Services here," Renee explained.

All the color drained from Allison's face. She was stunned. "Where's Jessica?" Allison screamed. "What have you done to my baby?"

Tom bit his lip. *The question is what have YOU done to your baby,* he thought. "For the moment, Jessica has been placed in a home where her safety is guaranteed. Your daughter is asserting that you are abusing her physically. Obviously, we will be looking seriously at her claim and in the interim, she will remain away from you."

"There may be formal charges filed against you, so if you don't have an attorney, you may want to obtain one. We will be back in the morning to get Jessica's things. You will be notified as things develop. Good night." Tom ended.

"Wait, please," Allison begged, but they were gone.

"I had to get out of there," Tom stated angrily. "As long as I live, I will never understand how a parent can do that to their own child."

"I know," Renee sighed. "Thank God Jessica has someone in her corner to fight with her - and for her. Most children aren't that fortunate."

"That's true," Tom agreed. They parted ways then, both leaving in their own vehicles but not before confirming a time to return in the morning for Jessica's things.

Allison slowly closed the door and leaned heavily against it. She was absolutely livid! What had that little brat gotten her into?! *I should have hit her harder! I had been too easy on her*! I shouldn't have let her go tonight. That's what I get for trying to be a good mother, she thought. *Well, I will teach her a lesson when I get her back here. No one will believe her story anyway. A seven-year-old over an adult? Forget it! She'll be sorry! Where was she?* Allison wondered. *That damn doctor had probably taken her somewhere.*

Allison remembered that Jason would be home in the morning. *What will I tell him? Well, it's his fault, anyway. He should accept responsibility for what he's done!* She picked up the phone angrily and dialed the hotel's number. Allison let it ring about 50 times. Then she slammed down the receiver. He had already checked out of his room. He was probably on his way home right now. She would tell him as soon as he walked in. She was furious with him for getting her into this mess! She walked upstairs and grabbed a suitcase from her closet. She threw it down on Jessica's bed and opened Jessica's drawer. Suddenly, she felt a pang. *What was that?* she thought. She felt it again. She stood staring at the empty bed.

I don't have to do this tonight, she decided. *I'll do it in the morning. I'm tired, yes, I'm much too tired to do this now.* Allison Ward walked into her bedroom and laid down on her bed. The moment her head touched the pillow, she fell asleep. It was not a peaceful one, though, but a restless, disturbing sleep. Allison heard the front door close and she leapt out of bed. She was still in yesterday's clothes. No matter. She quickly brushed her hair then ran downstairs. Her husband was putting his suitcases down when she appeared in the doorway.

"Jessica's gone," Allison said flatly.

"Gone? Gone where?" Jason asked, his voice filled with concern.

"Some agency took her, Jason. Evidently, she told her doctor that I hit her and they turned me in to the authorities." Allison stated dispassionately.

"What?" her husband screamed. He was shocked and angry. "Where is she Allison? Where is my daughter?" His emotions were completely out of control now.

"Shut up, Jason! I have no idea where she is. She left with Dr. LaMadrid yesterday afternoon and last night, a police officer and a woman from some agency came to say Jessica wouldn't be coming home right now." Allison said, exasperated.

"Why didn't you call me?" he asked.

"I tried," she retorted. "You had already left. And don't go getting all emotional now, Jason. They will bring her back soon. They'll know she's just making things up and that all I have done is discipline her, and only when she needed it." She sounded so confident.

"Oh God," Jason moaned, putting his face in his hands. "Why didn't I listen to her? I knew she was telling me the truth! I knew it. Now I've lost her, and probably for good!"

"Stop being so dramatic. She'll be home soon," Allison said, her voice reeking with sarcasm.

"Leave me alone. You make me sick!" Jason mumbled. "I don't know who disgusts me more right now, you - or me."

Jason left then and went into Jessica's room. He saw the open suitcase on her bed and began to weep. Why hadn't he done something? Why hadn't he made any kind of a move to protect his darling little daughter? He was so sorry, so very, very sorry. He picked up one of Jessica's stuffed animals and wept uncontrollably. He had never been more ashamed of himself. He had been great at providing Jessica with everything, everything but what she couldn't live without. Love, just love, and a little understanding. His beautiful little princess. Oh, how he had let her down! Wherever she was right now, she was in better hands than his own. He didn't deserve her. Not now. But he could change – he would change. *Please God,* he pleaded, *let me have just one more chance. I'll do it right this time, I promise.* He stayed in that room for a long while until he heard the doorbell. He jumped up a bit startled. *Jessica!* he thought. He raced to the door, threw it open, and stood unable to move. Standing there was a man and a woman. Once again, Tom and Renee introduced themselves.

Renee caught the pained expression on Mr. Ward's face but spoke firmly and directly, "We told your wife last night that we would be back to get Jessica's things. You will be informed of the court date for you to appear regarding these charges. Jessica is fine. Do you have her clothing ready?"

"I don't know," he seemed confused and disoriented. He was trying to absorb everything. "Please come in for a moment. I'll take care of it."

They stood in the living room, but just barely inside the doorway. *It was so quiet,* they both thought. They heard muffled voices coming from the kitchen then watched as Mr. Ward trudged up the stairs.

Jason put Jessica's clothing in the suitcase, keeping his emotions in check. He added her toothbrush, homework, and then gently closed the lid. Jason handed the suitcase to Tom then looked painfully at them both and said, "Please tell my daughter that I love her."

He gently closed the door behind them. "Why can't they ever do that before it has gone this far?" Renee asked angrily. Tom let out a sigh then said quietly, "I wish I knew."

CHAPTER TWELVE

EVERYONE PREPARES
FOR A CHANGE

Jessica opened her eyes slowly and saw Ernie looking back at her. For a moment, she smiled. *Oh,* she thought quickly. *I had better get back into that other bed.* As she stood up, she realized it was too late. Neither Albert nor Suzanne was in their bed. She tiptoed out into the hall way. Something smelled delicious. She was so hungry. She saw Suzanne cooking over the stove when she entered the kitchen. "Good morning, Jessica. How did you sleep?" Suzanne asked.

"Fine, thank you. And you?" she cautiously inquired.

"Oh, last night, I slept better than I had in many months. So did Albert," she mentioned casually. *Good,* Jessica thought, *they weren't mad at her for sleeping in their room.* For as long as Jessica would stay with Albert and Suzanne, she would sleep on the floor next to their bed. Albert would always leave the hallway light on and Jessica always silently crawled into her makeshift bed. She slept better on that floor than she ever had in her bed.

"Good morning, Jessica." Albert said. He was reading the paper in the living room. "Hi," she said, joining him. She felt totally comfortable with both Albert and Suzanne now.

Albert wanted to talk to her about what was going to happen to her. So he was glad when Jessica asked Suzanne, "May I help with something?" He wanted her to eat breakfast first, there would be time for the talk later.

"Sure! How about setting the table?" Suzanne asked. They had an enjoyable breakfast together. Albert smiled to himself as he watched Jessica eat. She had eaten 2 servings of everything and was on her second glass of milk. Another good sign. It hadn't escaped Suzanne either. She smiled knowingly at Albert.

"May I do the dishes, please?" Jessica asked.

"Oh honey, you don't have to do that," Suzanne felt a tug at her heart.

"Oh, but I want to, I really do!" Jessica exclaimed.

"Well, okay. If you're sure!" Suzanne smiled. "I'll just go and take a shower."

Albert wanted to help - it seemed to take her forever with only one hand, but he decided to let her do it by herself. She was so excited.

Wow, this is great! Jessica thought.

Albert went back to his reading and Suzanne treated herself to a nice warm bath then laid down for a little nap. Shortly before noon, Albert came in and gently awakened her. "Tom and Renee are back. They have Jessica's clothes. Do you feel up to talking with them?"

"Absolutely! I'll be right there." She threw some water on her face, brushed her hair, then joined the others in the living room. When Suzanne sat down on the couch next to Albert, Jessica (who had been standing up) walked over and with a little guidance from Suzanne, sat in between Albert and Suzanne.

Both put an arm protectively around her.

"Jessica," Renee began. "We need to talk to you for a few minutes. Do you feel up to it?"

"Yes, I'm fine." Jessica sounded more confident than she actually was.

"You were very brave to tell Dr. LaMadrid what has been happening to you. Your mother and father both need to get some help. There is never any right reason for anyone to hit a child. There's a problem deep inside that's being vented on you. We are going to ensure that this never happens again. Soon, your parents, you, Albert, Suzanne, Tom, and I will be going to talk to the judge. We are going to tell him everything. Then after he listens to us, he will decide what's best. Do you understand, Jessica?" Renee finished.

"Yes, I do. But do I have to go back home today?" she asked with tears threatening once again to make an appearance.

"No, honey. You can stay here, at least until we talk to the judge. Unless, of course, you don 't want to," Renee said.

"Oh, I do, oh please, I really want to stay." Then she drew in a breath, "Oh, I didn't even think. I'm so sorry." She turned to Albert and Suzanne saying, "I don't want to be any trouble for you. I can go somewhere else."

"Jessica, we want you to stay here with us more than anything. We really, really do." Albert said. Then they both looked directly at her and said, "Jessica, we love you."

Jessica could barely speak. "I love you both, too," she finally got it out. She hugged Albert then Suzanne. "Oh, and I have my bank book at home with over $100.00 in it. You can have it if you want."

All four adults chuckled then Suzanne told Jessica they had plenty of money and for Jessica to save her money for college. "You never know," Albert winked at Jessica. "You just may want to be a doctor yourself one day!" The mood lightened tremendously after that and they all conversed for a little while.

Renee left a little later but Tom stayed for a while. Albert told Tom they were going to have a baby. Tom was thrilled for his best friend. He knew how desperate they were to have a family.

Meanwhile, Suzanne helped Jessica unpack. They put her clothes in a dresser then Suzanne sat on the bed with her and brushed her hair. They talked about school and lots of other things, even boys. Jessica had never done that before. It was really fun.

Suzanne remembered the maternity clothes she had hid in the closet and brought them out to show to Jessica. "I need to start wearing them. I've outgrown all my other clothes," Suzanne chuckled. Jessica edged closer to Suzanne and picked up one of the new maternity blouses. She kept her eyes fixed on the blouse but said softly, "You are very beautiful."

"Oh, thank you," Suzanne was touched. She put her arm around Jessica and asked, "Will you still tell me that when I'm so big I can't get through the door?"

They shared a laugh together but after a moment, Jessica added, "Yes, I will, because it will still be true." Just then, the phone rang and Suzanne grabbed it. She had placed a call to her sister a few days ago but discovered she was out of town. She left a message asking her to return the call, saying only that she had something important to tell her. Suzanne spoke to her sister for quite a while. Marianne was very excited for her younger sister. "Oh, I hope it's a girl," she exclaimed. " I mean, if it's a boy, that will be great, too. But, oh, you know what I mean!"

"I know what you mean." Suzanne assured her. Marianne had 2 boys already; a 6-year-old named Eric and a 3-year-old named Derek. Last month, Marianne was told the child she was carrying now was a boy, too. Suzanne definitely understood. Suzanne told her older sister about Jessica and what she and Albert were embarking on.

"Gosh, I hope that little girl is going to be all right. Maybe we could come down and visit next week. Would that be okay?" Marianne asked.

"Sure, we would love it! Call me and let me know for sure when. Jessica and I will make dinner for you."

"I hope she's a better cook that you are!" Marianne laughed. "Of course you know I'm kidding. I love your cooking. Give my love to Albert, and tell him we said congratulations. We're all thrilled, absolutely thrilled!" They said goodbye and hung up. Suzanne went into the living room and discovered Albert helping Jessica with her homework. It warmed her heart. How wonderful it was to have a little person in their home. Jessica had a home here as long as she wanted.

They spent a leisurely evening together discussing how Jessica would get back and forth to school. "It was perfect," Suzanne said. Jessica's school was just a mile or so from where she taught so she could take her in the morning and pick her up, too!

Later that night, while she lay in bed, Jessica asked herself if she missed her parents. *She probably shouldn't feel this way,* she thought, *but she didn't miss them, not one bit. But I do miss Albert and Suzanne,* she decided. She crept noiselessly down the hallway with her pillow and blanket, and of course, Ernie. They laid down softly next to Suzanne and promptly fell asleep.

Jason and Allison were talking with their attorney and he was visibly upset. While Jason seemed contrite, wanting to know what kind of professional help they should seek and how soon it would be possible to begin, Allison seemed to show no remorse at all. They were to appear in court the following week. "Well, I guess that's it for now," Edward Munson said matter of factly. "I've arranged for us to meet with the judge privately. I'm not sure if your daughter, uh-"

"Jessica," Jason interjected.

"Yes, I'm not sure if Jessica will be there or not," he ended.

"Oh," Jason was genuinely saddened. "I really want to see her - even for a moment. Just to tell her that I'm sorry and that I love her." Allison stood mute.

"Well, we will let the judge know that we are beginning therapy immediately," their lawyer stated.

Then he stood up, looked at Allison, and said sincerely, "It's important to Jessica, and to you, Mrs. Ward, that you receive some help. Don't do this simply because you think this will ensure you'll get her back. It won't. Do it for yourself and for your family. Think about it, please."

"I will," she said slowly. Her husband looked at her. Was there a flicker of emotion? Perhaps the magnitude of what they had done had finally begun to hit her. Together, they walked to the door, Jason turning his back to utter a final thank you.

Edward Munson sat thinking at his desk long after the Wards had gone. Had he helped at all by saying that to Mrs. Ward? He really didn't know. He only knew he had to try. Edward picked up the phone, dialed his home, and when his 7-year-old daughter Jennifer answered, he said, "I love you."

When Jason and Allison arrived home a bit later, neither one wanted to walk in the door. It was so dreadfully quiet.

Jason sat in his recliner but did not relax. He couldn't stop thinking. How he wished he could turn back the clock. He would have never let it happen. He had learned a hard lesson. *I'm glad she told someone. I didn't listen to her. She called me begging for my help and I turned her away.* The tears began to stream down his handsome face. *If I ever get another chance with my daughter, I swear I'll hear her, I'll listen to her, and I'll love her. Not just when it's convenient for me, but all the time.* Oh, how he wished he had bought her that horse!

Allison walked into the room and found her husband crying. She sat down on the floor in front of him and looked him squarely in the eye. "Jason, I know I've done terrible things to Jessica," she began. "I'm as guilty as you are.

"I knew it. I think I've always known it. I just didn't want to see,"

"I should have known better. I let all the anger I have for you out on her. I know now that that was a reprehensible thing for me to do." I don't know why though. Why would I hurt my little girl? The only good thing I have ever done. I am glad I'm going to get some help, I really need it."

Then Allison stood and Jason saw a pained expression on her face. "Do you think we have lost her forever, Jason?" she asked.

"I don't know Allison. I don't know, " Jason's voice was heavy and sad.

CHAPTER THIRTEEN

STARTING A NEW CHAPTER

Jessica went to school on Monday and she appeared to be pretty much the same. She talked casually with Tamara and she studied her part in the Cinco de Mayo play. Albert promised to help her with her part also. She was excited about that.

Jessica was also afraid. Next Thursday, she would be going to speak with the judge. Of course, Albert, Suzanne, Tom, and Renee would go also; but still, it was frightening. She would tell the story once again. It still made her sad and mad. She loved staying with Albert and Suzanne though. They treated her so nice and they made her feel special. She tried not to think about the day when she would have to leave. She would just enjoy every moment of every day. These days, when she awoke, the first thing she did was say a little prayer of thanks.

The days passed quickly, not just for Jessica but for Suzanne and Albert as well. Before they knew it, that Thursday had arrived. No one needed an alarm that morning; all three had barely slept and decided very early to just get up.

"You're not eating your breakfast, Jessica," Suzanne commented softly. "Are you afraid of what's going to happen today?"

Jessica nodded. Suzanne covered Jessica's small hand with hers and said, "We are, too, sweetie. But remember, we are all in this together."

"I know, and I am so glad your both going with me." Jessica said.

Albert and Suzanne dressed silently and then all three waited impatiently for Tom and Renee. Albert had been so grateful to hear Tom say that he would be with them through the whole thing. He was also a very supportive friend. Finally, they arrived. Renee hugged Jessica and reminded her that the judge just wanted to talk to her and that she wasn't in any kind of trouble at all. In fact, just the opposite. They were all very proud of her. *The courthouse seemed so cold and impersonal*, Jessica thought.

As if reading her thoughts, Albert turned and said, "It doesn't look obvious but many good things happen here, too."

Jessica walked with Albert, with the doctor holding her cast gently at the elbow on the left. Suzanne held her right hand. *Suzanne looked so beautiful in her new maternity dress,* Jessica decided. Albert had remarked on it earlier as well.

They were told to have a seat outside the courtroom. After what seemed like an eternity, they were called in. Jessica looked everywhere for her parents but they were nowhere to be found. She wasn't sure if that made her happy or sad. Judge Reynosa was a distinguished look-ing man who seemed, to Jessica, about 8 ft. tall when he stood up. Jessica tried not to appear frightened. As he met everyone though, she relaxed just a little. He had nice warm eyes and he began by showing Jessica pictures of his grandchildren. I'll bet he is a wonder-ful grandpa, she thought.

He leaned over his cluttered desk and asked Jessica to tell him, in her own words, what had been happening and when it had all began. She started speaking slowly, stumbling over words, and clearly upset. How many times did she have to keep going over and over it? The judge listened intently but showed little or no emotion. Finally, it was done.

The judge said nothing for a moment, just leaned back in his chair. He let out a weary sigh then directed his gaze to Jessica. "Jessica, I will begin by telling you what a brave young lady you are. You should be very proud of yourself to realize inside you that you didn't deserve that treatment, and more importantly, to tell someone. Don't ever be sorry that you have done that!" he said sincerely.

"No, sir, Your Honor, I never will!" She stated candidly.

"That's good," the judge said, almost smiling. Then he grew serious again.

"Jessica, I spoke with your parents and their attorney earlier." Jessica felt her body becoming rigid. Suzanne and Albert tightened their grip on her and slowly, she relaxed. The judge continued, "Both of your parents are remorseful. Your father says that while he never witnessed your mother actually hitting you, he knew that she did. He regrets terribly not listening to your pleas for help." The judge took a deep breath. Even he was taken with this beautiful wide-eyed little girl. You just wanted to pick her up and hug her, and somehow make the pain go away. He couldn't, of course, so he proceeded. "Your mother has admitted to everything. She didn't deny a thing. She maintains that she doesn't know why she did it. We will leave that up to the experts, though. She has already begun receiving counseling this week. She will need to continue this therapy indefinitely. At some point Jessica, it will become necessary for you and your father to attend the sessions. Could you do that?"

"I guess so." She tried to sound convincing.

"Well, Jessica, it's important that you deal with your anger, too. If you are to be a family, it will require working together and also being patient. I don't want you to say or do anything right now. I'm going to ask you to come back in 3 months and we'll see how we're doing then. I hope your parents realize how fortunate they are to have a special little girl like you. When you come back, I will talk to you without your parents present so you can feel comfortable telling me whatever you feel. Does that sound okay?" the judge inquired.

"Yes," she mumbled. Then she began to cry.

"What is it honey?" Suzanne asked with concern.

"I don't want to go home. I want to stay with you and Zeus!" Jessica cried.

"Oh, Jessica, I'm sorry. You may stay with the LaMadrids at least until then. Renee says they're glad to have you, and I don't blame them. I should have told you. I'm sorry," the judge said apologetically.

Jessica brightened immediately. "That's okay. Thank you, Your Honor."

The judge looked at Albert, Suzanne, and Jessica - all three were beaming. He rose from his chair, extending his hand first to Jessica. "I believe one day we'll see great things from you, Jessica. You are a remarkable young lady. We'll see you in 3 months."

They all shook hands and then Albert, Suzanne, and Jessica thanked the judge profusely. All five of them shared a warm moment outside the courthouse. Then Tom and Renee left to go but turned and came back.

"Hey, Jessica," Tom wondered, "We couldn't quite make out what you called Albert when we were with the judge." Albert looked at Jessica, too. He hadn't understood either but had forgotten with all the other things going on. Jessica smiled at Albert and said unabashedly, "I call him my Zeus!"

Albert's eyes became moist and he swallowed hard to remove the lump in his throat. He picked Jessica up and said impassionedly, "I'm very flattered. I'll try my hardest to live up to that name."

"You already have," Jessica said sincerely. Jessica's days with Albert and Suzanne were nicer than any she remembered. She went to the hospital with Albert several times when he was making his rounds. She really enjoyed it, and she learned a lot, too. Maybe she would be a doctor! She did speak with her parents often, however. Her father was very emotional; her mother full of sadness, and what appeared to be a genuine desire to get well. Jessica didn't know whether to believe her or not. Soon, the day arrived for her to meet with her parents and the doctor. She was very apprehensive. Not that her mother would hurt her but just because she didn't want to even think about it anymore, much less talk about it.

Albert and Suzanne took her that afternoon and held her tightly before she entered the room. "Everything is going to be fine. You know you can trust us," Albert said softly.

He had been right the first time he had said those words, Jessica thought. That was very reassuring for her. She moved slowly, hesitantly, away from Albert and Suzanne. Then she placed her hand on the office door. Dr. Thouk, the sign read. She eased the door open deliberately, spotting her parents and the doctor seated inside. Jessica took a deep breath, garnered all her strength, and cautiously stepped inside.

64

THE END